In the Bible I can read
what God has to say.
How can I learn all I need?
Jesus shows the Way!

"Little children, come to me.
I will be your teacher.
Spread My love to everyone,
every living creature."

Jesus teaches me to love. He teaches me to pray.
I ask for help to be like Him, kind in every way.

When I follow Jesus' lead,
this is what I see,
I can love the whole wide world,
just as He loves me.

There are many super things that Jesus helps me learn.
I try my best to always share and wait to take my turn.

Jesus takes great care of me and gives me all I need. He helps me to know right from wrong, helps me to succeed.

Helping others helps me too. It's the way to grow.
When I follow Jesus' way, blessings overflow!

"Dear Jesus, thanks for family,
friends, and food, and play.
I know that You are always near.
You're just a prayer away."

I'm glad that Jesus is my Friend. I know He's here to stay.
I picture Jesus everywhere as I go through my day.

Now your child can discover the joys of following Jesus through *Picture Me™ with My Friend Jesus*. Just put your child's pictures in the frames provided and help your child experience the love and friendship of Jesus.

Written by Dandi • Illustrated by Carol Strebel

Look for these other inspirational stories...

Picture Me™ with Jonah and the Whale • Picture Me™ on Noah's Ark
Picture Me™ at the First Christmas

www.picture-me-books.com
PATENT #5,031,935

Printed in China.
10 9 8 7 6 5

PICTURE me BOOKS

ISBN 1-57151-541-0
0 99863 00541 3